The TALE OF BENJAMIN BUNNY

by
Beatrix Potter

Illustrated by
Tim Kirk

Troll Associates

Library of Congress Cataloging in Publication Data

Potter, Beatrix, 1866-1943.
    The tale of Benjamin Bunny.

    SUMMARY: Peter's mischievous cousin, Benjamin
Bunny, persuades him to go back to Mr. McGregor's
garden to retrieve the clothes he lost there.
    [1. Rabbits—Fiction] I. Kirk, Tim. II. Title.
PZ7.P85Tak 1981   [Fic]   80-27468
ISBN 0-89375-484-6
ISBN 0-89375-485-4 (pbk.)

The TALE OF
BENJAMIN BUNNY

One morning, a little rabbit sat on a bank. He pricked up his ears and listened to the *trit-trot, trit-trot* of a pony. A carriage was coming along the road. It was driven by Mr. McGregor, and beside him sat Mrs. McGregor in her best bonnet.

As soon as they had passed, little Benjamin Bunny slid down into the road. He set off with a hop, skip, and a jump to call upon his relations, who lived in the wood at the back of Mr. McGregor's garden.

That wood was full of rabbit holes. In the neatest, sandiest hole of all, lived Benjamin's aunt and his cousins—Flopsy, Mopsy, Cotton-tail, and Peter.

Old Mrs. Rabbit was a widow. She earned her living by knitting rabbit-wool mittens and muffs. (I once bought a pair at a bazaar.) She also sold herbs, and rosemary tea, and rabbit-tobacco, which is what we call lavender.

Little Benjamin did not very much want to see his aunt. He came round the back of the fir tree, and nearly tumbled upon the top of his Cousin Peter. Peter was sitting by himself. He looked poorly, and was dressed in a red cotton pocket-handkerchief.

"Peter," said little Benjamin, in a whisper, "who has got your clothes?"

Peter replied, "The scarecrow in Mr. McGregor's garden." Then he described how he had been chased about the garden, and had dropped his shoes and coat.

Little Benjamin sat down beside his cousin. He assured him that Mr. McGregor had gone out, and Mrs. McGregor also—and certainly for the day, because Mrs. McGregor was wearing her best bonnet. Peter said he hoped that it would rain.

At this point, old Mrs. Rabbit's voice was heard inside the rabbit hole, calling, "Cotton-tail! Cotton-tail! Fetch some more camomile!" Peter said he thought he might feel better if he went for a walk.

They went away hand in hand, and got up on the flat top of the wall at the bottom of the wood. From here, they looked down into Mr. McGregor's garden. Peter's coat and shoes were plainly to be seen upon the scarecrow, topped with an old hat of Mr. McGregor's.

Little Benjamin said, "It spoils people's clothes to squeeze under a gate. The proper way to get in is to climb down a pear tree."

Peter fell down headfirst, but it was of no consequence, as the ground below was newly raked and quite soft. It had been sown with lettuces.

They left a great many odd little footprints all over the ground—especially little Benjamin, who was wearing clogs.

Little Benjamin said that the first thing to be done was to get back Peter's clothes, in order that they might be able to use the pocket-handkerchief. They took the clothes off the scarecrow. There had been rain during the night, so there was water in the shoes, and the coat was somewhat shrunk.

Benjamin tried on the hat, but it was too big for him. Then he suggested that they should fill the pocket-handkerchief with onions, as a little present for his aunt.

Peter did not seem to be enjoying himself. He kept hearing noises. Benjamin, on the contrary, was perfectly at home, and ate a lettuce leaf. He said that he was in the habit of coming to the garden with his father, to get lettuces for their Sunday dinner. (The name of little Benjamin's father was old Mr. Benjamin Bunny.)

The lettuces certainly were very fine. But Peter did
not eat anything. He said he should like to go home.
Presently, he dropped half the onions.

Little Benjamin said that it was not possible to get back up the pear tree with a load of vegetables. He led the way boldly towards the other end of the garden. They went along a little walk on planks, under a sunny, red brick wall. The mice sat on their doorsteps, cracking cherry-stones. They winked at Peter Rabbit and Benjamin Bunny.

Presently, Peter let go of the pocket-handkerchief again.

They got among flowerpots, and frames, and tubs. Peter heard noises worse than ever. His eyes were as big as lollipops! He was a step or two in front of his cousin when he suddenly stopped.

This is what those little rabbits saw round that corner!

Little Benjamin took one look, and then, in half a minute less than no time, he hid himself and Peter and the onions underneath a large basket.

The cat got up and stretched herself and came and sniffed at the basket. Perhaps she liked the smell of onions! Anyway, she sat down on the top of the basket. She sat there for *five hours*.

I cannot draw you a picture of Peter and Benjamin underneath the basket, because it was quite dark, and because the smell of onions was fearful. It made Peter Rabbit and little Benjamin cry.

The sun got around behind the wood, and it was quite late in the afternoon. But still the cat sat upon the basket.

At length, there was a *pitter-patter, pitter-patter*, and some bits of mortar fell from the wall above. The cat looked up and saw old Mr. Benjamin Bunny prancing along the top of the wall of the upper terrace. He was smoking a pipe of rabbit-tobacco and had a little switch in his hand. He was looking for his son.

Old Mr. Bunny had no opinion whatever of cats. He took a tremendous jump off the top of the wall onto the top of the cat, and cuffed it off the basket, and kicked it into the greenhouse, scratching off a handful of fur. The cat was too much surprised to scratch back.

When old Mr. Bunny had driven the cat into the greenhouse, he locked the door. Then he came back to the basket and took out his son Benjamin by the ears, and whipped him with the little switch. Then he took out his nephew, Peter. Then he took out the handkerchief of onions and marched out of the garden.

When Mr. McGregor returned about half an hour later, he observed several things that perplexed him. It looked as though some person had been walking all over the garden in a pair of clogs—only the footprints were too ridiculously little! Also he could not understand how the cat could have managed to shut herself up *inside* the greenhouse, locking the door on the *outside*!

When Peter got home, his mother forgave him, because she was so glad to see that he had found his shoes and coat. Cotton-tail helped Peter fold up the pocket-handkerchief. Then old Mrs. Rabbit hung the onions from the kitchen ceiling, along with the bunches of herbs and the rabbit-tobacco.